THE ADVENTURES OF
ROCKY
AND
BULLWINKLE
MOVIE
JOKE BOOK

SIMON SPOTLIGHT
An imprint of Simon & Schuster Children's Publishing Division
1230 Avenue of the Americas, New York, New York 10020

Copyright © 2000 Universal Studios Publishing Rights, a division of Universal Studios Licensing, Inc. The Adventures of Rocky and Bullwinkle and friends and related characters are trademarks and copyrights of Ward Productions, Inc. Licensed by Universal Publishing Rights, a division of Universal Studios Licensing, Inc.

SIMON SPOTLIGHT and colophon are registered trademarks of Simon & Schuster.

Manufactured in the United States of America
First Edition   2 4 6 8 10 9 7 5 3 1
ISBN 0-689-83326-1

THE ADVENTURES OF
ROCKY
AND
BULLWINKLE
MOVIE
JOKE BOOK

DIRECTOR

BULLWINKLE

by David Lewman

Simon Spotlight

New York   London   Toronto   Sydney   Singapore

Rocky: Bullwinkle's back!

Bullwinkle: And my front's here, too.

Natasha: Which kind of fish keeps falling apart?

Boris: Broke trout.

Why can't Minnie Mogul sign a contract that will help three bad guys take over the world?
Her pen's out of ink.

What has antlers and sleeps for twenty years?
Rip Van Bullwinkle.

Rocky: What's that loud crashing I hear early every morning?

Bullwinkle: Must be dawn breaking.

Boris: How do I send message to a wolf?

Natasha: Use fox machine, dahlink.

Why did Boris use a computer to control his weapon?
He wanted to kill a moose with a mouse.

Why does Bullwinkle talk to trees?
He's in charge of Wildlife Conversation.

Natasha: What is Pottsylvanian hospitality?
Boris: That's ability to put you in hospital.

Cappy Von Trapment: Allow me to be frank . . .

Bullwinkle: Okay, I'll be Bullwinkle.

Is Karen Sympathy's prison-guard boyfriend young?

No, he's Ole.

Why did Bullwinkle take a picture of his hands?

He wanted to snap his fingers.

What do you call a trial about a stolen cushion?
A pillow case.

What do you call a trial about a stolen hamper?
A basket case.

What do you call a trial about stolen underpants?
A brief case.

Rocky: Why did you put that
can of corn on the police
officer's head?
Bullwinkle: I wanted
corn-on-the-cop.

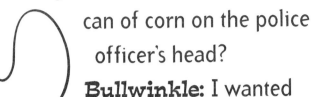

**Why did Boris drop the heavy
locker on Rocky and
Bullwinkle?**
He wanted to play it safe.

**How did the chicken cross the
canyon?**
In a heli*coop*ter.

**How did the werewolf cross the
canyon?**
In a *howl*icopter.

Cappy Von Trapment:
This note gives Karen
the job of rescuing a cat.
Bullwinkle: I see . . . it's
purr-mission slip.

**Why did the
pumpkin buy a
uniform?**
He wanted to be a security
gourd.

**How do you get a lady
off a catwalk?**
Whisker off!

Rocky: What do you do when the water around your castle dries up?

Bullwinkle: Use the re-moat.

What do TV characters eat out of?

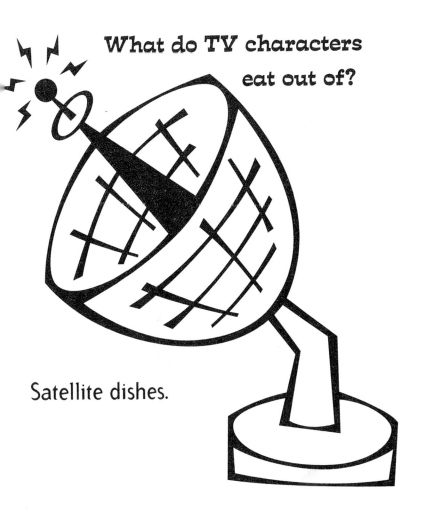

Satellite dishes.

Rocky: Bullwinkle, why do you think America would smell better if we drove all the time?

Bullwinkle: Because then we'd be one big car-nation!

Why did Bullwinkle pour water in his car?

He wanted to start a car pool.

What did Bullwinkle use to pour water in his car?

Bucket seats.

Why did Bullwinkle throw coins in the river?

He wanted to change the channel.

Which channel can never be changed with a remote?

The English Channel.

Rocky: Why did you give that hive a present?

Bullwinkle: I wanted to make my honey happy.

What do bees use to comb their hair?
Honeycombs.

What did the snake say after being treated to lunch?
"Fangs for the bite!"

Why did Bullwinkle drill a hole in his head?
He wanted to keep an open mind.

Does Bullwinkle like archeology?
Yes, he digs it.

When does Bullwinkle disagree with everybody?

When he's playing Mr. No-it-all.

Why did Rocky go into space?

He wanted to be an astro*nut.*

What's the opposite of antlers?

Unclers.

Rocky: Where do Egyptians deposit their money?

Bullwinkle: The banks of the Nile.

What happened when Bullwinkle ran into the trap?

He really put his foot in it.

Natasha: Could you be even worse, Boris?

Boris: No, I'm *Badenov*—ha, ha!

Why did Bullwinkle dig a trench on the football field?

It was a last ditch plan.

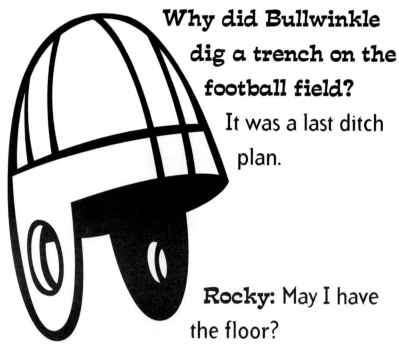

Rocky: May I have the floor?

Bullwinkle: Only if you promise to give it back.

Rocky: How can we enlarge the membership of our fan club?

Bullwinkle: Get them to eat more.

Rocky: Why do quarterbacks do well in school?

Bullwinkle: They know how to pass.

Why did Natasha think the football game was broken?

Because Boris said he'd fixed the game.

Natasha: Did you go to Penn State?

Boris: No, State Pen!

Bullwinkle: I won't take this sitting down, Rock.

Rocky: Why not?

Bullwinkle: Because they just painted the chairs.

How did the baseball player escape from prison?
Three strikes and he was out.

Did Bullwinkle do well selling vacuums?
Yes, he cleaned up.

Why should you never give a balloon ride to your centipede?
Because that's putting all your legs in one basket.

Rocky: Where can I get a book on plants, flowers, and trees?

Bullwinkle: The branch library.

What do you get when you cross Boris and Natasha's boss with a frog?
Fearless Leaper.

What has antlers, six eyes, and fights with swords?

The three *moose*keteers.

Natasha: How is cannon factory doing, dahlink?

Boris: Business is booming.

What does Boris always order with his hamburger?
Squirrelly fries.

Bullwinkle: Why are the drinks so small in Frostbite Falls?
Rocky: Because they're in Mini-soda.

Rocky: What happened when the jelly truck tipped over?
Bullwinkle: There was a traffic jam.

Why isn't Bullwinkle afraid of an avalanche?

Because rolling stones gather no moose.

Why does Boris use so much shampoo?

He's trying to get the moose out of his hair.

How does Bullwinkle keep his messages secret?

He uses moose code.

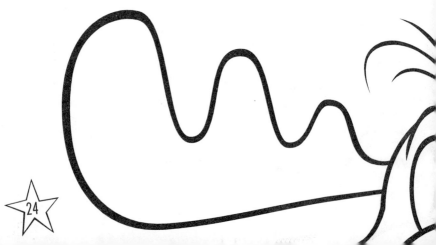

What's Bullwinkle's favorite disguise?
A big black *moose*tache.

What has antlers, wings, and likes to bite people?
A *moose*quito.

Which beauty pageant did Bullwinkle win?
The Moose America Contest.

How does Bullwinkle keep up with what's going on?

He reads his daily *moose*paper.

What does Bullwinkle get when he's scared?

*Moose*bumps.

What do you call a moose after a long bath?
Bullwrinkle.

What happened when Bullwinkle's friend fell out of a tree?
He hit Rock bottom.

Which baseball team does Bullwinkle's friend root for?
The Rockies.

Why did Bullwinkle take his friend to the park?

He wanted to see a Rock slide.

Rocky: Bullwinkle, why do you keep making these terrible jokes?

Bullwinkle: I can't help it—I'm under a gag order!

Why did Wossamotta U. recruit Bullwinkle for its football team?

He had all the right hooves.

What did Rocky say when the ice rink burned down?
"Hockey smoke!"

Why did Miss Fatale tie her hair up tight?
She wanted to be Knottasha.

Knock, knock.
Who's there?
Boris.
Boris who?
Bore us with one of your stories—we could use the sleep.

What did the beaver say when Boris stole his log?

"You took the woods right out of my mouth!"

Why did Bullwinkle plop ice cream on Boris's head?

He wanted spy à la mode.

Which tree has the strongest bark?

The dogwood.

Why did Rocky leap from a doorknob?

He wanted to fly off the handle.

Knock, knock.

Who's there?

Acorn.

Acorn who?

A corny joke is better than none!

Bullwinkle: Hey, Mr. Tree, why are they cutting all the woods down?

Mr. Tree: I don't know . . . I'm stumped!

Why do moose grow antlers?
They like to rack their brains.

**What does Rocky keep
important papers in?**
A nut case.

**Which kind of nut goes best with
toast?**
The butternut.

**Which kind of nut
is full of treasure?**
The chestnut.

Which part of Rocky is like a shrub?

His bushy tail.

Why does Rocky walk through the woods backward?

He likes to follow the tail.

Does Bullwinkle like it when Rocky flies?

Yes, because then he has friends in high places.

How are Rocky and Bullwinkle like baby plants?

They're buds.

How did Bullwinkle do in the Big Face contest?

He won by a nose.

Where did Rocky get his coat?

He won it fur and square.

What does Rocky do if a spark falls on him?

Calls the fur department.

Knock, knock.

Who's there?

Minnesota.

Minnesota who?

Minnie sorta lost the keys—open up!

Can Rocky be scary?
Yes, he can be quite fur-rocious.

Why did Bullwinkle try to pull a rabbit out of a chest of drawers?

He thought it was a hare-dresser.

Why did the two young hairs hate combs?

They couldn't stand to part.

What happened to Bullwinkle's carrots?

They vanished into thin hare.

What's the difference between Rocky and your uncle's wife in a boat?

One's a rodent and the other's a rowed aunt.

Rocky: Did you have fun last night, Bullwinkle?

Bullwinkle: Oh, yeah, I was the laugh of the party.

What did Bullwinkle say to the captain of a really ugly ship?
"Eye, eyesore!"

Why did the funny car stop running?
It ran out of gags.

How did Bullwinkle survive the shipwreck in the grocery store?
He landed on a dessert aisle.

Rocky: What do you get when you cross a Great Dane with a German Shepherd?

Bullwinkle: Great Danger.

Bullwinkle: Rock, I thought the conductor said I could play in his band.
Rocky: No, he said when it comes to playing, you're banned.

Why did Bullwinkle hit home plate with a stick?
He wanted to play the base drum.

What does Bullwinkle's friend do first thing in the morning?

He gets off to a Rocky start.

Why did Bullwinkle carve a sphere out of wood?
He wanted a beech ball.

Why did Natasha keep saying "ding" at the dance?
She wanted to be the bell of the ball.

Rocky: Bullwinkle, why are you carrying that saw?
Bullwinkle: You said we'd take a bough at the end of the show.

Why did Bullwinkle pour oil in the stream?
Because it had a creak.

Why did the pool ball go back to the table?
He missed his cue.

Who ran Cinderella over with a boat?
Her ferry godmother.

Rocky: Why do chimneys cough out smoke?
Bullwinkle: Because they've got the flue.

Bullwinkle: Which one of Robin Hood's men was chicken?

Rocky: Fryer Cluck.

Bullwinkle: Why did George Washington always sleep standing up?

Rocky: Because he promised
he'd never lie.

**What do you give
a brave robot?**
A metal.

What did Bullwinkle say when the puddle evaporated?

"He'll be mist."

Why did Bullwinkle try to squeeze milk out of rock?

He'd heard it came in quartz.

Why did the boat get smashed by the dock?

It gave in to pier pressure.

Natasha: What was it like when Fearless Leader dropped window on you?

Boris: A real pane in the neck!

Natasha: You are sneaking into bakery disguised as muffin?

Boris: It'll be my greatest roll.

What did Bullwinkle say when the shoemaker offered to put new bottoms on his boots?

"Soled!"

Is it hard to change cattle's minds?

No, a cow is easily suede.

Rocky: What happened when you told your joke?

Bullwinkle: It got so quiet you could hear a pun drop.

Why did Bullwinkle put a frog in his cap?
He wanted to pull a ribbit out of his hat.

How do rabbits defend themselves?
Karate hops.

What did Bullwinkle say when he kept pulling a lion out of his hat?
"Here's my mane problem."